The Legend of Papa Noël

A Cajun Christmas Story

Written by
Terri Hoover Dunham

Illustrated by
Laura Knorr

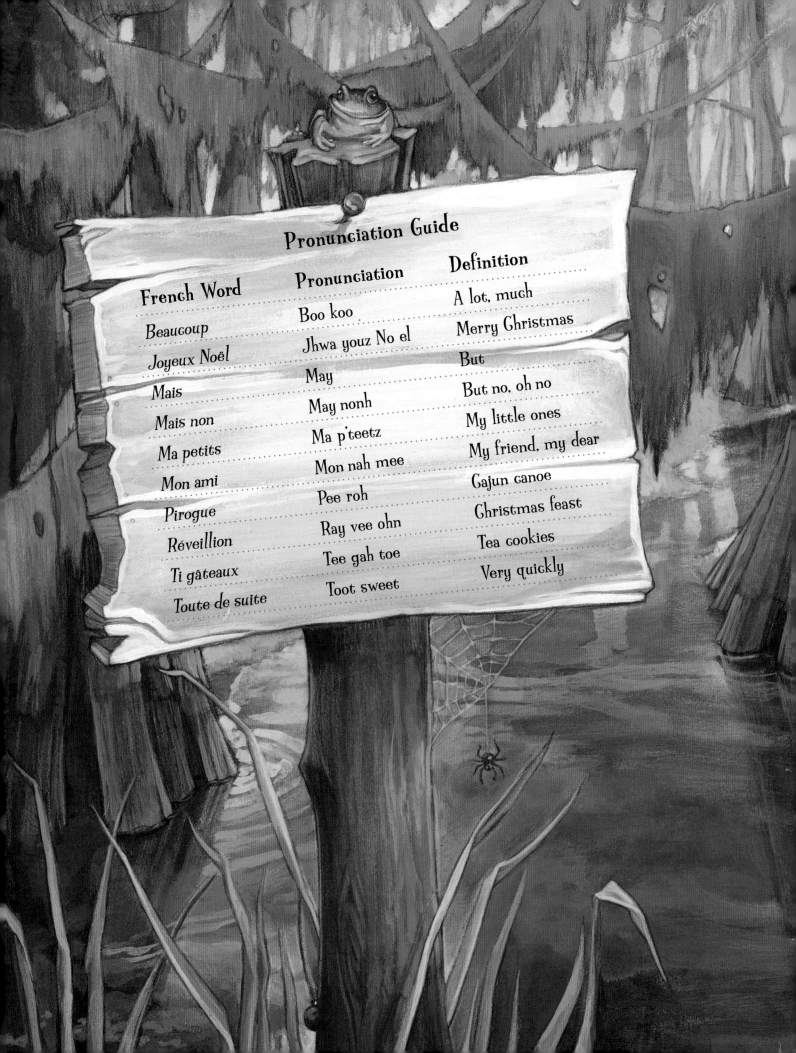

Pronunciation Guide

French Word	Pronunciation	Definition
Beaucoup	Boo koo	A lot, much
Joyeux Noël	Jhwa youz No el	Merry Christmas
Mais	May	But
Mais non	May nonh	But no, oh no
Ma petits	Ma p'teetz	My little ones
Mon ami	Mon nah mee	My friend, my dear
Pirogue	Pee roh	Cajun canoe
Réveillion	Ray vee ohn	Christmas feast
Ti gâteaux	Tee gah toe	Tea cookies
Toute de suite	Toot sweet	Very quickly

So what if all them childrens in the city calls him Santa Claus! In that place called England, he's knowed as Father Christmas. And over yonder in France, he goes by Père Noël. Sure, he's got more names than you can shake a stick at. But in Cajun country, we call him Papa Noël. Do you wanta hear a story about that little old man? *Mais* you know, I'm just about to tell you one.

That Papa Noël, he lives so far back in the deepest, darkest swamp in Louisiana that not even the bravest Cajun fisherman will go there. And that is exactly how that fella likes it, peaceful and quiet. You know, he's gotta think real hard when he's making that list and checking it twiced. He's really gotta use his noggin when he gets to carving all them little toy *pirogues* and baby dolls outta cypress knees. Then when Christmas Eve finally gets here, he's gotta count them things before he loads up his *pirogue*.

But that Papa Noël, he don't get too lonely out there, 'cause he's got them nine pet alligators to talk to and they real smart, even talk back some. Now that Étienne is a little too smart and he talks back *beaucoup*.

So Papa Noël, he spends all year long making them toys for the good little Cajun boys and girls. And on Christmas Eve he goes right down that Mississippi River to deliver them.

Ah, but one Christmas Eve while Papa Noël was stuffing them toys into that big burlap sack, he saw something he didn't like.

"*Mais non!* Jus' look at dat fog rolling in! It thicker than gravy on rice!" he said as he throwed that bag in his *pirogue.*

Well, Papa Noël knew that fog was getting thicker by the minute and pretty soon he wouldn't be able to see how to hitch his alligators to the front of that *pirogue.* So, he worked as quick as a squirrel runs up a tree.

First he fixed Étienne and Émille to the *pirogue*,
then Remmy and Renee in front of them.
Next, he tied up Alcée and Alphonse,
then François and Fabienne.
And leading that team was Nicollette.

Now Nicollette was full of a certain kind of magic. You know how alligators are all green and how their eyes glows red at night? Well, Nicollette was as white as powdered sugar and her eyes shined green like kerosene lamps. But on that Christmas Eve, the fog got so thick Papa Noël was not sure her magic was enough.

"Mon ami, Nicollette, I don't tink even your magical eyes will get us tru dis fog. But we must try. Ma *petits* await der toys!"

Papa Noël shouted as they began their trip down that foggy river.

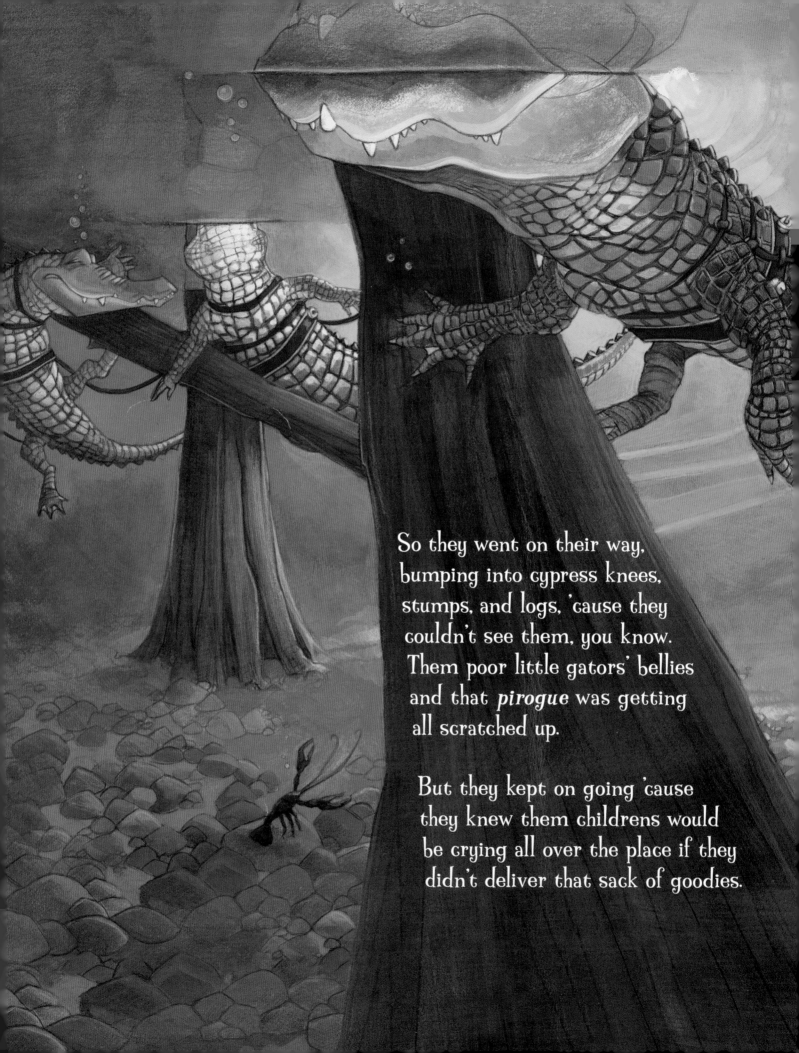

So they went on their way,
bumping into cypress knees,
stumps, and logs, 'cause they
couldn't see them, you know.
Them poor little gators' bellies
and that *pirogue* was getting
all scratched up.

But they kept on going 'cause
they knew them childrens would
be crying all over the place if they
didn't deliver that sack of goodies.

Then, after a while of going along
like that, Étienne hollered,

"Mais, Papa, we must stop, *toute de suite!*
I know my hide is tough, yeah,
but my belly is hurting! I can't go on like dis!"

So Papa Noël climbed outta his *pirogue* and waded through that muddy water. And he patched up that gator's belly with some moss and duct tape. Then they went on their way again.

Oh they tried to weave in and outta them stumps and logs. Nicollette hitted them first, then she turned her head and hollered at the others, "Swim left, turn right!" That way, they missed a lot of them bruises, yeah. But poor Nicollette was getting pretty scraped up. And it was taking so long to go just a little ways!

Well, that Étienne hollered, "We won't never make it! Dis night is half over and we ain't got to one house yet!"

Ah, but just then they
rounded the bend and they
saw something just over yonder
that was a glowing like gold.

"Wh-what's dat?"

Étienne hollered.

Well, they couldn't see what was causing
that strange light, but pretty soon they could
make their way down that river just fine. That
light shined right down on that muddy water
and made it sparkle like it had some of them
diamonds in it. Then quicker than a nutria runs
from a gator, they had made it to that spot.

"Mais, look at dat!"
Nicollette said.

So all them alligators and Papa
Noël, too, raised up them heads
to see what she had done seen.

You see, Cajuns is some kinda
smart, yeah.

When they seen that fog rolling in, they knew Papa Noël would have trouble getting to their houses. And they knew they wouldn't be able to find their way to church for Christmas service in all that thick stuff. So, they put their noggins together and figured out exactly what to do.

Them mens went out and chopped them up some willow logs and gathered some cane reeds. They worked *beaucoup* hours stacking that wood up and by the time they finished, there was a string of bonfires all along that levee. Then them mens all got home, put on their Sunday clothes, and headed off to church, with them bonfires lighting the way.

"Dem bonfires is halfway up to dat sky.
And der must be a hundred of dem!"
Étienne squealed.

"I shoulda figured dem Cajuns would know what to do,"
Papa Noël said. "Now we can see dem houses wit no problem.
Ah, but enuf of dis talk. We got some kinda work to do, yeah!"

Then quicker than a snake shimmies down the river, they
got themselves to the first Cajun house. And Papa Noël
and his gators could see that the *Réveillion* feast
was through 'cause them lanterns had done been snuffed out.

So, they started delivering all them toys
to the good little Cajun boys and girls.

Time went by fast as they went up and down that river and in and outta them houses. Papa Noël was quicker than a frog hopping across a log, putting all them toy *pirogues* and cypress dollies under them Christmas trees. But he slowed down just long enough at each house to have him a couple *ti gâteaux* and some of that eggnog them Cajun childrens left for him. And he read all them letters they wrote, too.

Then, with their job all through, Papa Noël
and his gators left the last house. And as
they was going, Papa Noël hollered,

"Joyeux Noël to ya'll!
And to ya'll a good night!"

By the light of them bonfires, they went on their way back to Papa Noël's cabin, deep in the darkest part of that swamp.

And when they got there, all tuckered out from delivering all them little toy *pirogues* and cypress dollies, they went fast asleep, just like them little Cajun boys and girls.

For my loving husband, Ronny, and my beautiful, beloved sons, Ryan and Brett.
And to my wonderful mom, Blanche Hoover. I could not have done it without your
love and support. Thank you for believing in me.

In memory of my father.

Terri

For my mom, whose strength and love inspires me, now and always.

Laura

Sleeping Bear Press™

2395 South Huron Parkway, Suite 200
Ann Arbor, MI 48104
www.sleepingbearpress.com

Printed and bound in the United States.

10 9 8 7 6 5 4 3 2

Library of Congress Cataloging-in-Publication Data

Dunham, Terri.
The legend of Papa Noël : a Cajun Christmas story /
written by Terri Dunham ; illustrated by Laura Knorr.
p. cm.
Summary: This Cajun version of Santa's Christmas Eve deliveries
tells of Papa Noël living in a Louisiana swamp and bringing
gifts in a boat pulled by alligators along the Mississippi River.
ISBN 1-58536-256-5
[1. Christmas–Fiction. 2. Santa Claus–Fiction. 3. Louisiana–Fiction.]
I. Knorr, Laura, 1971- , ill. II. Title.
PZ7.D92077Le 2006
[E]–dc22   2006004772